Short Stories No.2

The Director

By

Sean De Siun

art camino

fiction

Published October 2020
by Art Camino

This is the second in a series of short stories.

This book is a work of fiction any resemblance to events or
people past or present is absolutely amazing, but is wholly
a product of the author's imagination.

A CIP record for this book is available
from National LIbrary of Australia

ISBN 978-0-9806049-7-9

COPY SALES
The Director is available on **amazon.com**
Purchase direct from **artcamino.com/fiction**

Distribution enquiries:
Art Camino Fiction

sales@artcamino.com

1

Kieran and Cheryl walked arm in arm along Killiney Strand. As it was June, the evening twilight lingered with tinges of red in the swirling high clouds and dappled blue-green waves flopped on the pebbly beach.

'Darling, I'd much prefer it if you came to London with me tomorrow. London is fantastic in the summer and there will be parties and people to meet,' said Cheryl.

'Ah no Cheryl, this summer I need seclusion. I will do as I've planned and go to West Cork. I've not had a real break for ten years. This is my opportunity to reconnect with nature, my nature. More importantly I have to go over the shooting script in fine detail. I need to know it back to front and I have to liaise with Zak. I can't have any distractions.'

'So you will miss the London summer? I bet you won't last three weeks.'

'You know Josh has offered me his house at Inisheen and "I shall have some peace there. For peace comes dropping slow".'

'Really Kieran, you in the countryside, all secluded? What will you do except go mad? I am sure you'll find a local girl, or more likely a backpacker from Sweden to flirt with. I cannot imagine you all alone in boring peace.'

'It's peace I must have now. Besides, I do have to work. Zak will be in Bantry. You know we start shooting in September.'

'Months of work with our wedding in December, no honeymoon. You should come to London with me. It will be our last chance for us to be together for ages.'

'But Cheryl, you'll be working in London. At night you'll be going to parties, drinking, eating. That is exactly what I don't need at this time - distractions. I must prepare myself physically and mentally.'

'Ha, as I said, you'll find someone there to distract you without me there to look after you!'

'Don't be like that, darling. We'll have plenty of time together soon enough. You must concentrate on your work and don't have too much fun. A stint at the National Gallery will do your career a world of good. When the shoot is over, we'll be together full-time.'

'You won't make it through the summer. I'll tell everyone you're coming to London later. But you go and do your Buddha thing.'

'Are you sure you want me in London with you? Maybe you'll enjoy your time without me. When we're married you won't be able to get rid of me at all. "Whenever you look up I'll be there, and whenever I look up you'll be there".'

'Kieran, I love you, but don't try to scare me off. Maybe you are right, absence makes the heart grow fonder. But you'll miss a great summer all the same.'

They reached the north end of the beach and climbed the steps up to the crossing over the train tracks and into Vico Road.

Kieran was fortunate that his work brought him into contact with the glitterati of the Irish film and entertainment industry. Well, glitterati in Ireland, not necessarily Irish. Ireland was a prime film location for big film productions. Big stars, producers and directors had houses on the Southside of Dublin near Killiney.

His friend Josh Blinden was a Hollywood producer and had rented a big place on Vico Road. On a previous trip to Ireland he had bought a 'small get-away' in West Cork. Josh now offered him the house for the summer. One other mutual friend, a painter called Henry, would be going down as well, but probably not for a few weeks.

Kieran and Cheryl walked up to the imposing gates of the house and the security guard waved them in. Josh was having evening drinks on the lawn.

They mingled with a small crowd of people in the industry and sipped champagne as the red sky finally turned dark blue, with the Sugarloaf Mountain turning to a dark silhouette at the south of Killiney Bay past the town of Bray.

It was Friday evening and, as Keiran and Cheryl often did, they wandered down Vico Road after the party to Sorrento Road and into

Dalkey to eat at their favourite Italian restaurant. After dinner they had a drink in the Dalkey Duck.

'Let's go over to Liam's. He's having a session tonight,' said Kieran. They took a taxi to Liam's place in Ballybrack. The door was unlocked and they climbed the stairs to his flat. Inside, musicians sat in a semicircle with others dotted around with various instruments from fiddles to ukuleles, a saxophone and guitars.

The crowded, smoky room was abuzz with lively conversations and laughter. Soon one musician picked up a guitar and began to play, then another joined in and then another. Liam sang and played his guitar until the whole room was playing a part. Kieran shook a tambourine and Cheryl banged a bongo drum.

In the early hours of the morning, Kieran and Cheryl finally pulled themselves away as the session continued, and walked the short distance to their flat in Shankill. Thus ended a typical weekend night for them in South Dublin.

The next day Kieran put his suitcase on the back seat of his Toyota Corolla and Cheryl's bag in the boot, and drove Cheryl to the airport. After they kissed goodbye he continued down the M7 and M8 to Cork City and then he took the N71 through Bandon, Clonakilty and Rosscarbery. As he entered West Cork he deliberately slowed the car down. I had better get into West Cork time, he thought. Down here the time is always 'about half-past'.

He admired the rugged but lush green hills dotted with purple heather and yellow gorse as he slowly drove through Skibbereen to Ballydehob. He continued on down Mizen Peninsula, the most southerly of the five peninsulas that finger out into the North Atlantic. After leaving the town of Schull he caught a glimpse of the Fastnet Rock with its distinctive lighthouse far off the coast, alone, surrounded by sea.

He opened his window to take in the country smell as the car brushed by thick hedges of flowering fuchsia. When he reached Goleen, he stopped and went into the pub to ask directions as Josh had advised him to do. The road to the house at Inisheen, Goleen, near Skibbereen was very secluded, he had been told.

Sometime later the publican came out to the street followed by Kieran and waved his arms pointing up the hill, then down the hill, gesticulating and speaking quickly in a West Cork accent that Kieran could hardly understand at all.

'Many thanks, I think I'll be grand now sure. I'll be back soon... no I won't be a stranger not at all... sure I will... ah sure grand... and thanks again... I will, I will... fine day it is... grand day for driving yes... God bless... your wife too...'

'I thought I'd never get away,' he muttered to himself as he attempted to decipher the convoluted instructions he'd been given.

After only a few wrong turns he came to a crest in the steep, narrow, unsealed road and there he saw the house – Inisheen. Beautiful aspect, he thought as he looked down into the bowl-shaped depression in the hills. At the bottom stood a large stone house surrounded by fields and dry stone walls. The rocky hills climbed one hundred feet or so in three directions and the road ahead passed over another shallower crest on the southern side and disappeared down towards shimmering water below. Beautiful place. Just what I need. Pity I won't have it to myself. But beggars can't be choosers.

He drove up to the house, went in and started to make himself at home. Six weeks of peace and solitude in this lovely house at the southerly tip of Ireland. Bliss. The first thing to do was to make sure the wifi was connected. Ah, super-fast. That's typical – a better connection in the wilds of the country than in town.

Kieran had been living in a small flat above a convenience store but not for much longer, or so he hoped. He had finally secured a major project after ten years of working his way up in the industry. He had been chosen to be Assistant Director of a major film that was going to be shot in the Wicklow Mountains and at Ardmore Studios in Bray. If it went well, as he was sure it would, maybe one day he would end up in a big house on Vico Road, or in Malibu.

He would be working with the Director Zak Flender who was spending the summer working at a house near Bantry not far from Inisheen. At some point in the next few weeks, Kieran would be summoned to meet with him there. The rest of the time he and Zak would go back and forth on the script with notes and emails. He hoped he would only have to work for an hour or two a day. He wanted to spend the rest of the time relaxing and getting mentally fit.

The next morning he woke up early, before sunrise. He climbed the hill on the eastern side of the road and took in the magnificent view, looking northeast as the first rays of the morning sun shone gently on the islands of Roaring Water Bay. The bay was dotted with islets within a convoluted coastline of green and rocky hills. His eyes followed the sunshine as it bathed the coast and the Fastnet that shone like a pearl in the sea. He turned in a full circle with views all around.

Below the sheer cliffs in front of him was the perfect natural harbour of Crookhaven. He could see the village on the other side of the harbour with three pubs and a few houses. Turning south, he looked towards Mizen Head, the most southerly tip of Ireland. To the west he could see across to the Beara Peninsula and the North Atlantic Ocean beyond. He clambered back down to the house and made breakfast.

I am going to completely change my schedule, he told himself. This is the first time I have seen the sunrise for many years apart from when I am getting home from a night out. Kieran normally slept late and either worked or partied until the early hours of the morning.

He determined that he would drink little, eat less, swim in the sea and rise at dawn every day. I am going to read, not just the script, but books, he said to himself with conviction. The large living room in the middle of the house was lined with bookshelves. He cast his eye across them, Proust, Balzac, Zola. Perfect inspiration for any filmmaker. I'm going to meditate and go to bed at ten.

Pleased with his determination to be good and lead a healthy lifestyle for the summer, he pulled a volume off the shelf and sat down to read. I had better be bloody good, he thought, I cannot afford to stuff this job up or I won't be marrying beautiful Cheryl or moving to Hollywood.

He read and wandered around the house and surrounding fields. By mid-morning he had tired of the book and was about to check his email.

Bang, crack, the front door burst open. Henry fell into the room pulling a large roller bag. 'Hi Kieran, good to see you,' he shouted. 'This is a great place isn't it? Wait a minute. I'll get a bottle from the car.'

Seconds later Henry was back brandishing two bottles of Paddy. 'Time for a drinkie-poo eh Kieran? Two lads down south for the summer. We are gonna have some fun, aren't we!'

'Henry, no, no, no. I came down here to rest and work.'

'This is resting. Relaxing with a bottle of whiskey, the best thing for you.'

Surprised by Henry's sudden appearance, Kieran asked, 'What are you doing here anyway? I thought you weren't arriving for weeks.'

'My wife is working shifts, six nights a week, and she needs some space. There's nothing going on in Dublin and the weather is looking great. So I thought I'd come down early. So come on, relax and have a drink with me.'

'Henry, in Dublin I drink all the time, smoke, carry on. I have to get fit and together. I want peace. No drinking for me.'

'Well, Kieran, if I knew you were gonna be like that I would have gone to Malta or Greece. I'm having a drink anyway. I need one after the drive.'

'I thought you were coming here to paint?'

'I am going to paint – tomorrow, or later in the week maybe. I can't bloody well paint all day can I? I'm also going to go to the pubs in Crookhaven and there are parties planned at some of the houses roundabout. It's going to be a classic West Cork summer. There will be music, champagne and women.'

'No women. Definitely no women, Henry.'

'Well actually, there will be at least one woman. A young woman, in fact, and she's very nice indeed I understand. Josh called me last night. He met a girl in Dublin, you know, they had a thing. He said she could stay here and we wouldn't mind at all.'

'When is she arriving?'

'Tomorrow, I think.'

'Good God. My summer is ruined. You know I have no will power. I had to get away or I would be a wreck by the time we start production.'

2

Keiran awoke as the first rays of the sun shone through the window of his bedroom. Oh, the second day and I have already broken my vow to watch the sunrise. He clambered out of bed and sat in the alcove of his window. The house was built in the pre-famine Irish style of dry stone walls nearly a metre thick with stucco on the outside. The window made a wide bench to sit on and look out to the heather, gorse and rugged rocky terrain.

I'll see the sunrise – or nearly! He rushed up the cliffs and turned full circle as the newly-risen sun bathed the landscape in golden rays. Clouds over the ocean to the west danced towards the Irish coastline but looked friendly and benign in the warm summer air. It's going to be a lovely day, he thought and smiled to himself. Now, I must get to work on the script.

He once again clambered down the cliff and made porridge and stewed apple for breakfast with lashings of hot lovely tea. After breakfast, he opened his laptop on the dining table and checked his email.

Subject: Where Are Y ou?

Damn it Kieran I have been up for two hours sending you notes on the script. Where the hell are you? Get back to me soonest.

Zak

Shite, the bastard is either on drugs or winding me up. He hurriedly replied to the email.

Zak, I'm on deck now, sorry to be late. Reading your notes now.

K

He hurriedly read through the seven emails from Zak containing numerous changes, observations and questions about the first page of the script.

Two hours later after frantically working through his responses, he stopped to make himself a jug of coffee.

'Top of the morning, Kieran,' Henry shouted, striding into the kitchen from his bedroom in a loosely fitting dressing gown.

'Henry, do your gown up, will you? I am seeing much more of you than I ever want to again,' said Kieran averting his eyes from Henry's hairy legs and chest.

'Oh sorry, Kieran. I forgot how sensitive you are. I should have remembered from when we were at college.'

Henry strode up to the kitchen counter and turned on the radio.

dum da la dum dum dum... RTE News ... The Taoiseach has announced sweeping new reforms to school crossing zones across Ireland ...

Henry then grabbed the TV remote and switched it on.

da da de de da da... BBC News ... The British Prime Minister today released a plan for sweeping reforms ...

'HENRY, turn that bloody racket off NOW!' bellowed Kieran.

'Wha's up wit yas, Kieran? I'm just making me breakfast. Bad hair day, is it?'

'Henry, I was here first. I'm here for peace, so I can work. Don't mess with me, man. You are here to paint. So go and paint. From now on I don't want to see you or hear you or drink with you.'

'Well all right, if that's the way you want it, you tight arsed bastard.'

Aggrieved, Henry tightened his gown, unplugged the radio, nestled it under his arm, raised his nose and marched back to his room.

Kieran opened the back door and went into the garden. He sat at the table and collapsed his head in his arms. What an enervating start to the day. Now I must meditate. He forced himself upright, closed is eyes and his mantra began.

Effortlessly his mantra sprang, again, again, no effort, not trying to think, no thought. Finally, he felt relaxation, a serenity came over him. He felt detached from his fiance, from Zak, Henry. Now he felt he could be productive and work.

'Hello, am I disturbing you?' said a sweet voice.

He opened his eyes to see an auburn-haired girl smiling at him. She was lovely, youthful with vibrant eyes and a gentle smile.

'Are you a vision?'

'Hardly, I'm your housemate, Kayley.'

'Hello, Kayley. A delight to see you nice and early in the morning.'

'What are you doing here sitting all alone?'

'I'm meditating, contemplating the cosmos, you understand – getting ready for the day ahead.'

She was tall with pale green eyes and pouty lips. She looked at him as if he were a source of amusement. She had mischief in her eye, or so he perceived.

'Well, I've just driven up from Cork City. Do you mind if I make myself a cup of tea?' she said and strode off into the kitchen. Kieran followed her. She was beautiful, but he was annoyed at her presence, disturbing his desired peace.

'You came from the city today, Kayley?'

'Yes, from my parents home. I was there for a few days. It's summer holidays now so I can relax a bit.'

'Are you working or studying?' Kieran asked.

'I just graduated from UCD. I hope I'll get a job in September.'

'Ah, what subjects?

'English, Drama and Film.'

'Very good, the same course as I took when I was your age,' said Kieran.

Kayley smiled at him, 'So you were my age once?'

'Never I was. I mean I went to UCD as well. But I'm here to work. So, although the three of us are here together, perhaps we can agree to keep apart. So I can work, you know. I must have peace and solitude, so please don't be offended if I rather ignore your presence.'

'You must have very important work to do?'

'It's important to me.'

'Really? What are you up to down here in West Cork?'

'I'm reviewing the script of a movie that we're shooting in September.'

'Is that right? Well, I shall try my best to leave you to it.'

Kayley turned away and opened the kitchen cupboards to see what each one contained. She found a bowl and poured muesli into it.

'Well I'll see you around I guess … what's your name, anyway?'

'Me? I'm Kieran.'

'Nice to meet you Kieran, I suppose,' said Kayley as she turned her back on him again and strode out into the garden.

Kieran followed her into the sunshine. The kitchen faced west and puffy white clouds danced overhead, dappling sunshine and shadow on the hills and crags.

'Where is my bedroom?' she asked.

'Come, I'll show you and you can choose.'

The original stone building had two rooms on the ground floor and two rooms above. But Josh had greatly extended the house, adding new rooms to each side. It now had five large bedrooms, each with an en suite bathroom.

'This is my room,' said Kieran as he waved at a closed door at the top of the stairs. This room is Henry's where he is sulking after I was mean to him, and there are three more bedrooms down the corridor. Take your pick.'

'I think I'll take the one that is furthest away from your room,' said Kayley.

'Very sensible, but I'm more worried about you biting me than you should be worried about me biting you,' said Kieran.

3

Kieran left Kayley to settle into her room and went downstairs into the open plan living and dining room where he had set up his computer to work. He heard creaking from Henrys' car boot and a dragging sound.

Henry set up his easel in the garden and began to paint. Kayley joined him and they talked and laughed. Keiran became fascinated by Kayley. She was so self-confident. As she chatted with Henry she didn't seem overbearing or shy. She was serene, mature.

I've got to get away from them, he told himself. I must keep on the straight and narrow. He put on his swimming trunks, picked up a towel and left them to it, driving to the beach at Barleycove for a swim.

I'm just going to ignore them both assiduously, pretend they are not there. My life is going to change one way or the other. I won't be going back to the 'scene' in Dublin, that's for sure.

The wide sandy beach was nearly deserted when he arrived. He splashed in the surf for as long as he could stand the cold water. The sun sparkled through the dappled clouds. The breeze coming from the south was warm. The salty ocean smell reminded him of being with Cheryl walking along Killiney Beach.

He sat on the sand for a while and then decided to head back to the house to do some work. As his car turned into the narrow driveway, a car pulled out and nearly hit him.

'Sorry!' the young male driver shouted as he reversed the car back so that Kieran could drive in. Kayley was on the front seat next to him, laughing. As soon as he was in the driveway the car sped away tooting twice on its way out. Kayley waved her hand out the window at Kieran.

Henry was still painting in the garden out the back. Although he had decided to ignore his two housemates, Kieran was curious. He went into the garden, and asked, 'Henry, who was that?'

'I don't know, Kieran. Some fella arrived and beeped his horn. The next thing, Kayley was running out the door.'

'Did you talk to her much?'

'We did have a nice conversation indeed.'

'What do you make of her?'

'Agh, she's just a young woman out for a good time. What do you expect?'

'Nothing, I guess. She's good looking all right.'

'Not bad at all, very pretty. You're not thinking of having a go are you?'

'No no not at all. I have to work, as I keep saying. Straight as an arrow I must be.'

'Come off it, Kieran. What's with all this Mr Serious stuff? It's not like you at all. You're the life and soul of the party.'

'Not now Henry. I have an opportunity here. I'm going to change my life. I'll be successful.'

'Well, you've lined up your trophy wife and landed this job. But that doesn't change who you are. They'll see through you eventually.'

'Stop, Henry. We're not so young any more. You think of me as the wild youth. I'm growing up, maturing.'

'Ha, rather ripening like an old cheese! Have you finished work for the day?'

'I guess so, there's nothing more I can do until Zak fires off a million questions for me at four in the bloody morning. I thought I would be very quiet and read through the script.'

'Come on, don't be silly. I can see you need to shake off some of your fear. You seem very nervous, Kieran. I'll drive – let's go to Crookhaven for a pint.'

Kieran gave in. It was true that there was nothing much he could do until he received more instructions from Zak. But one little drink will be all right, he told himself. I'll start work in earnest tomorrow.

As Henry's car passed over the top of the hill and down the steep road to the coast below, the Fastnet shone like a jewel in the sea. Crookhaven was a deep and narrow inlet. The village of Crookhaven consisted of three pubs around a square with the harbour on the fourth side, a few houses and a church. There was a stone harbour wall for small fishing boats and a fisherman's co-op.

Henry parked the car and they went into O'Sullivan's Bar. A slogan painted on the wall outside read 'The Most Southerly Pint in Ireland'.

'Two pints of Murphy's, please', said Henry.

They took their drinks outside and sat at a table overlooking the harbour. 'See across the way, Kieran. On the top of that cliff. That's where Inisheen is.'

On the mainland side of the inlet was a sheer rock bluff about 300 ft tall. At the base was a buttress and old constructions.

'What is that, Henry?'

'It's an old copper mine. Marconi made the first-ever radio broadcast across the Atlantic from here. He chose this location because he needed copper to make his radio transmitter.'

'Well, there you are Henry, a mine of information.'

'My family used to come down here for the summer when I was a kid. We stayed at Barleycove. It's a beautiful spot. We came here to Crookhaven to buy mackerel, straight off the fishing boats. You never tasted better fish in your life. Sláinte,' he said, lifting his pint of stout to his mouth.

They sipped their beers and admired the view. Two beers later, the sun was getting low in the sky. But it was mid-June and summer solstice was just a few days away, so it would not get dark until after 10 pm. They relaxed as the long twilight unfolded.

More people came for a drink, and by the early evening it was quite lively. A session started up and Irish music wafted out from the pub opposite O'Sullivan's.

'Cheers Kieran, hic, it's great to see you again. It's been a while since we tied one on together.'

'Too long all right, Henry.'

'Tell me, Kieran. How did you land this job anyway? The last time we talked you were Assistant Director of Photography.'

'In truth Henry, it was a bit of a try on, a confidence trick. That is, I gave them confidence in me, misplaced confidence. I was working on the final series of 'Return of the Viking'. The director needed someone to look

13

after the second unit that was shooting extra scenes up at Powerscourt and in the Wicklow Mountains. I made up a story that I had directed a prize-winning short film and got the gig. To my amazement when the series came out I was credited as one of two Assistant Directors.

'Then I was approached by Zak Flender's people who were looking for an Assistant Director for this show.'

'What is the movie you are going to make called again?'

'That's the thing that got me the job, Henry. It's called 'Vikings: Zombies Awake'.'

'Zombie Vikings. You're kidding?'

'Not at all. I'm sure it's going to be a smash hit. Because of my credit on 'Return of the Viking' and experience shooting in Ireland and Wicklow, they thought I might be suitable. The other assistant director who had worked on Vikings wasn't available so they called me. However, Zak wanted to hear my ideas and see if I would be able to work with the Director of Photography and the rest of the team. That's where the auld charm came in.

'I read everything I could about Zak, the DP and everyone else involved with the project and I constructed a story that made it seem that my ideas jelled with theirs perfectly.'

'Good man, well done. Do your ideas jell with theirs?'

'I don't have any ideas at all. I never had it mind that I would direct. Sure, I hoped to be DP one day ... in a few years maybe. But they gave me the job and I've been running to catch up ever since. I don't have much confidence that I can pull this off.'

'Go 'way, Kieran. You'll be fine, no worries at all. If you can bluster your way into a position like this it demonstrates that you are capable.'

'We'll see. Assistant Director is possibly the worst job there is. I'll get the blame for every stuff-up. If takes are not up to scratch, it will be down to me. If we don't meet our deliverables schedule, my fault. If the movie is a success, all the credit will go to Zak.'

'Well drink up old boy, leave your troubles at the bar. The night is young. Let's go inside and see who's around.'

By now the whole village had turned into one big pub party. Customers from the three bars strolled from one to the other. It was like one establishment with an outside area. It was a beautiful evening and the sky turned orange, then an ever-deepening blue until well after 10 o'clock when the stars finally came out.

Laughing, joking and singing, it was like a family get-together. Everyone acted as if they had known each other for years, even if they had never met.

'Hey, long lost friend! What's your name again?'

'Hic, I'm Kieran and this is Henry.'

'That's right,' said the fellow that Kieran had never laid eyes on before. 'How's your father?'

'Ah sure he's grand he is, I'll let him know you were asking for him. What's your name again?'

'Johnny O'Sullivan from Drinagh. This young man here is my cousin Brian. Over there is his brother and sister, and over there are our cousins from Kerry.'

'Is it a family reunion you're having?'

'Not really, it's just that whenever we come to Crookhaven there seem to be a lot of O'Sullivans around.'

Kieran and Henry mingled and drank until after midnight when Henry said, 'Kieran, I'll leave the car here and we can walk home.'

'Walk? It's too far.'

'We'll be all right. It's not as far as it looks, just a few kilometres.'

They stumbled around the coast road and up the hill back to Inisheen. Kieran glanced at the clock as he fell into bed and saw it was 1:30. Oh God, I have to get up in a few hours.

He was sound asleep until woken by loud crashing and doors banging. He heard Kayley laughing and the sound of kissing. Two pairs of feet climbed noisily up the stairs and crashed into Kayley's room. The unmistakable sounds of passionate lovemaking kept Kieran awake. He covered his head with his pillow and drifted back to sleep.

'Kieran, Kieran! Your phone's been ringing repeatedly for an hour. It might be the boss, you had better answer it,' Henry shouted at him.

He opened his eyes and there was Henry once more in his dressing gown with his hairy chest and belly bulging out. 'Oh, my head hurts. What time is it?'

'It's 9:30.'

'Oh no, no, Zak will kill me.'

He pulled himself together and made coffee. He went to his computer on the dining table and checked his email. Sure enough, about a dozen emails had arrived from Zak. The last one read –

I need reliability. If I cannot depend on you to be working when I am, you are no use to me. WHERE ARE YOU?

Er, er, he picked up his phone. 'Hi Zak. Sorry, I had a bit of an emergency, yes, yes I know, er. OK, you're right but you know, an emergency…'

Henry was in the kitchen that opened onto the living room and smiled when he heard Zak bellow,

'I DON'T CARE IF YOU'RE ON A SINKING SHIP. YOU'RE WORKING FOR ME. BE THERE WHEN I NEED YOU GODDAMIT.'

'OK, OK, it won't happen again. I can promise you. I ran out the door to handle an emergency and left my phone behind. In future, no matter what, I will be there whenever you call. I'm onto it now, goodbye.'

A few minutes later Kayley and her boyfriend came downstairs and proceeded to make breakfast, smiling at each other with knowing eyes.

'You don't look too well, Kieran. Were you working all night?' she said with a smirk.

Determined to stay calm and project an air of professionalism, he said, 'Kayley, you are disturbing me. I came here to work and for peace and quiet.'

Henry, Kayley and her friend all burst into laughter. Realising the hopelessness of his situation, he unplugged the power cord from the wall, picked up his computer and mouse and took them to his bedroom. This will have to be my living space from now on, he told himself.

He had taken the master bedroom. It had a large picture windows looking into the back garden and the surrounding hills as well as the alcove that looked out to the driveway.

A short while later he heard two toots of a car horn and the screech of wheels and engine roar. Kayley had gone out with her boyfriend. He spent the rest of the day replying to Zak's emails. At the end of the afternoon, he felt satisfied that he could do no more until the next barrage from Zak. Henry was painting in the garden and he went to the kitchen for something to eat. He was pleased to have a quiet evening and went to bed exactly at 10pm.

He was woken from his sleep once again by a loud noise as Kayley and her friend thumped up the stairs for another sex session. Awake and tormented, he covered his head with his pillow but, as he was sober, it didn't work. He lay awake listening to them until their bed at last stopped creaking. He glanced at his watch – it was 2 am.

His phone alarm woke him at 5:30 and he checked his email before making coffee. Thanks be, no emails from Zak. So he is human after all, he thought. However, an hour later the emails started and Kieran set to work.

Mid-morning, he made some more coffee, went into the garden and sat down across from Henry with his back to the kitchen door.

'Top of the morning to you, Kieran. Fine day, is it not?'

'Fine day it is for sure.'

He felt relaxed. Perhaps this will work out after all. If I can keep Henry at bay and Kayley is either in or out with her boyfriend all the time, I should be able to get through this, he thought.

A few minutes later Kayley came into the garden followed by her boyfriend. Henry looked up and his jaw dropped. Kieran wondered what he was staring at and swivelled around to look. His jaw dropped as well. Kayley was with a different boy this time.

'Good morning, gents,' said Kayley. 'This is my friend, Michael.'

'Good morning, Kayley and Michael,' Henry and Kieran said in unison.

This boy lasted two nights. But on the third morning, he drove off leaving Kayley behind. A few hours later Kieran looked up from his computer to see a new car come into the driveway. A young man stepped out of a Mercedes as Kayley ran out to meet him. She threw her arms around him and they kissed. They got into the car and the Mercedes slowly exited and made its way out of Inisheen.

My God, what an operator she is, he thought. She is a very popular girl. He couldn't work anymore. He was getting used to the torment of listening to her lovemaking. Last night he lay in bed with his eyes wide shut imagining that it was himself in her bed, in her arms, beneath the sheets drinking in her musky scent. With each sigh, he felt it was he that was giving her pleasure. He heard the boy moan and he felt the tingling sensation as if she were caressing him.

Now that there was a third boy, he couldn't stand it. He felt like a tragic Greek character, tortured anew each day. He went to talk to Henry in the garden. 'Did you see that, Henry?'

'She went off with her boyfriend, I guess.'

'Her new boyfriend it was.'

'What a third bloke? She is a tiger, isn't she? Have you heard her making love every night?'

'How could I not hear it? I'm being driven crazy.'

Sure enough that night Kieran was woken again, this time after Kayley and her friend were already in bed. With this boy she was quiet, he could hardly hear them at all. This fellow seemed a bit less boorish than the other two. It made him despise him even more.

Now, he didn't imagine him in his place. No, he pictured himself as the indignant lover discovering his mistress in bed with another man. He would storm through the door and pull him off of her. 'Get out you wretched dog,' he would say and watch the blackguard drive away meekly in his bloody Mercedes, his hands on his hips and a menacing glare in his eyes. It would be best to shoot it day for night, yes, and black and white. Humm, what lens would I need? Then he would seize Kayley and ravish her.

He created a complete scenario. The story ended as he and Kayley left from the harbour at Crookhaven, standing on the back of a fishing boat with the rugged captain in his Aran sweater, pipe in mouth, winking and saying, 'Don't you two lovers worry, we'll reach the coast of France before morning.'

They would embrace as the sun set behind them, a light mist drifting across as the boat pulled slowly away from the camera, fade to black, roll credits. Yes, 'Gone with the Sea', Directed By Kieran Coakley ASC. ... Academy Awards, BAFTA.

His phone rang, twillip, twillip, 'Hello, yes Zak, I am awake ...'

4

Keiran put down his phone and looked over the two pages of notes he had written while talking to Zak.

Well, at least I know what I have to do. He breathed a sigh of relief. No more waiting. He had much to do and his thoughts raced forward to getting on set and out into the Wicklow Mountains to shoot the movie.

He was responsible for all second unit filming. This involved a variety of shots. He would direct the filming of empty backgrounds that the digital versions of the Viking village and actors would be composited into later. He would also direct the crowded battle scenes that did not involve the principal actors. One scene had thousands of zombie Vikings marching up a hill, down another and storming castle walls. Extras would be placed at intervals around a large field with trackers on them, marching back and forth. The VFX crew would then use software to fill in all the gaps with computer-generated characters to give the impression of a multitude of zombies. He was also responsible for many of the secondary green screen shots that would be used with the backgrounds in the final composite.

Zak would concentrate on directing the scenes with the principal actors.

It was very complicated work planning for all the eventualities that might occur. It was too expensive to figure everything out on set with dozens of paid crew standing around. The starring actors would only be available for a specified number of days before flying off to their next show. Every detail had to be worked out before any money was spent on set. A team of people, with Zak at the head, had been working out the complex details for months.

Now all the arrangements were being finalised. After the six week semi holiday in West Cork, Kieran would spend August at Ardmore Studios working with the VFX supervisor before the actors and production crew arrived in September.

Kieran sent his replies to Zak's long list of questions. It was 2 pm and he sat back in his chair and relaxed with the rest of the day to himself.

The front door slammed and he heard Kayley run up the stairs and close her bedroom door. She's home early, he thought. She had been with Mr Mercedes for three nights and they seemed very happy together each morning at breakfast. But she was alone now.

Last night he had managed to sleep without interruption. But now he was grateful for the intrigue that Kayley had brought. Inspired, his wild dream from a few nights before had solidified into a movie idea. He was working on the story in the afternoons when he had finished on Zombie.

It was a romance, of course, set at Crookhaven and surrounds. If Zombie is a hit, who knows, maybe this will go somewhere, he thought.

The first week at Inisheen had not turned out as expected, but he was now feeling settled in.

He looked out the window and saw Henry working on his painting. He went downstairs to join him.

'How's the painting coming along, Henry?'

'Not bad. What do you think?'

Kieran looked over the large canvas. The hills were a red colour and the trees and shrubbery a funny orange and yellow. The stone walls were an otherworldly green, 'Overall, Henry, it is strangely compelling, even beautiful.'

'Thanks, I appreciate that. It is a semi-commission. An art dealer in Dublin said he could sell as many of this type of painting as I could do. I hope to get five grand for this one.'

'Very good. Did you hear Kayley come in? She was alone.'

'Yes, the Mercedes man dropped her off. Could that mean a peaceful night?'

'Maybe, or perhaps there's another fella on the way over right now. How do you think she has the energy not to mention the mental capacity for so many men in her life?'

'Well Kieran, I think she's just young. She's doing what we would do if we had the chance. Never turn an opportunity down, especially not a romantic opportunity.'

'True enough. I've had my share of short term romances. That's all I have ever had, just not so close together.'

'Until now that is, eh? I mean you're engaged to Cheryl.'

'Yes I am engaged. Somehow I haven't thought of Cheryl for days. In fact I'd forgotten all about her.'

'You've been dreaming about Kayley, I bet.'

'Not at all!'

'Well I bloody well have been. Every night, imagining me in her arms. Seriously, Kieran. I can see the way you look at her. You're every bit as interested in her as I am. More than I am – I have my wife waiting at home. I'm in no need of any attachments – not even one night stands.'

'Henry you're wrong, I'm not the slightest bit interested in her. She's not my type at all. Besides she is probably ten years younger than us. Intellectually, physically, emotionally, we're not suited at all.'

'Well, that is pretty definitive all together. If you're not interested, then, I dunno, maybe I am after all.' Henry smiled, looking Kieran directly in the eyes.

Kayley came out of the kitchen hands in the back pockets of her jeans. She looked relaxed, less tense than she had been with her boyfriends. 'Hello fellas, let's see the painting. Humm, interesting use of colour Henry.'

'You're back early, Kayley. Are you going out again?' said Henry.

'No, nothing on tonight. My friend's gone back to Dublin.'

'What about your other friends? Will you be seeing them again?' asked Kieran.

'No, they were just boys I met down here, didn't go anywhere.'

'Too bad,' said Henry, 'But you know what day it is, don't you both? It's summer solstice, midsummer night.'

'So it is. Shall we all dance naked around a campfire?' said Kayley.

'Now you're talking. That's a great idea. But I have a genuine idea for us to celebrate the day,' said Henry.

'What do you have in mind?' said Kieran

'I'll show you some of the sights of this area. We can have a look at a few Celtic monuments and drive down a couple of the peninsulas.'

'Sounds good! Let's go,' said Kayley.

'First stop Mizen Head, the most southerly tip of Ireland.'

Keiran sat in the back and Kayley in the front beside Henry. Kieran already regretted what he had said to Henry. Not interested in her? He was fascinated by her. After all, he was writing a starring role in a film for her character. He looked at Kayley's profile as she turned to talk to Henry.

Great shot, he thought. He planned it all out in his mind. The front windscreen would have scenes of Paris at night with lights flashing as they drove past La Coupole and down the Champs-Élysées. He figured out how to light the inside of the car to make her look like Ingrid Bergman.

Henry drove them all around the Mizen and Sheep's Head Peninsulas. They stopped periodically to take in the beautiful scenes. Henry and Kayley talked animatedly and laughed at each other's jokes. Kieran felt left out and stared out his window as the countryside kaleidoscoped past. He felt like excess baggage being dragged around as he opened his car door and stepped out to look at yet another breathtaking sight. Henry and Kayley had already run to the top of a rocky lookout without even looking to see if Kieran was still there. After a while, they ran back and jumped in the car and Henry started to drive off.

'Hang on, Henry!'

'Oh, sorry, Kieran. I thought you were still in the car.'

Henry drove quickly along the narrow twisting roads. Kayley put her hand on his knee affectionately and Henry glanced knowingly into her eyes.

'Is she really falling for Henry?' Kieran wondered. Deflated, he opened his window to feel the rush of cool, fragrant summer air. A sense of failure filled him, of being left out.

Henry parked the car at a tea shop near the end of the Sheep's Head Peninsula. 'Let's have tea and scones,' said Henry as they stepped out of the car. 'Kieran, you go ahead and order for us. Kayley and I will have a look at the view.'

Kieran ordered a pot of tea for three and chose three slices of cake from the display cabinet.

'That makes 45 Euro,' said the German serving girl. The Italian waiter said, 'Here, a table has just become free, please to sit. You will have a pleasant view of the ocean.'

Soon the waiter brought over the pot of tea. Kieran looked at the ocean waves crash on the cliffs below. A few hundred yards away Henry and Kayley stood on a rock ledge. Henry put his arms around Kayley and they kissed.

You bastard Henry, damn it. Kieran turned his head away. He looked again and they had disappeared. Fifteen minutes later they emerged in the distance clambering over the rocky spine of the peninsula.

They made their way into the cafe and drank a cup of cold tea and ate their cake in silence, looking into each other's eyes oblivious of Kieran.

He felt abandoned, alone, by his own design. He had spurned Kayley, pushed her away from him. Henry had even offered her to him, and now he was left behind.

'Let's go home and spend the evening gazing at the stars,' said Henry to Kayley, his eyes soft like a puppy's, his hand in hers.

Back at the house, Henry pulled a pot-belly stove out of the shed and into the garden.

'I'll make a nice turf fire,' he said to Kayley.

Kieran slunk off to his room with a bottle of whiskey. He looked out of his bedroom window at the two of them, sipping his drink. Kayley and Henry sat gazing at the fire, entwined in each other's arms as the evening twilight slowly turned to a bright star-filled night. The warm glow of the crackling turf shone across their faces. They looked happy, in love.

He woke up with a start, his head in his arms on his desk, the whiskey bottle in front of him nearly empty. He rubbed his face and shook his head. Looking out the window to check on the two love birds, he could only see the soft dying embers glowing in the stove. Henry and Kayley had gone.

'Well, that's that, blown it, disaster,' he cried out as he stumbled onto his bed and crashed asleep.

Despite his hangover, he forced himself out of bed at 7:30. Thankfully, there were no emails from Zak. Maybe he had a mid-summer night party as well, he thought. He was still in his clothes from the day before. He had a shower and went downstairs to make breakfast.

While he was eating his cereal Henry emerged from his room in his dressing gown. He hastily wrapped it around himself more fully and tightened the chord.

'Good day to you, Kieran. If you don't mind I will quietly make some breakfast so as not to disturb your morning meditations.'

'Of course, Henry. Go ahead. How does Kayley like her eggs?'

'I'm only making breakfast for myself.'

'I'm surprised, you two were getting on so well last night.'

'True enough, but she's not ready for another relationship. She says that she respects me. I'll have another go today.'

'Oooh, respect. That's a bad sign. Looks like you're out of the picture, my old boy!'

'As I said, I'll keep at it.'

Kieran felt a wave of relief sweep over him. A smile took over his face. He stretched his arms and picked up his mug of coffee. 'Ah, I feel great today. Nothing from Zak, the weather is beautiful. It's going to be a wonderful day,' he said as he sprang up and took the staircase two steps at a time to get back to work.

There was still nothing from Zak so he started to work on his story. The title had changed from 'Gone With the Sea' to 'From There Through Eternity'. He banged away at his keyboard until lunchtime.

Why am I so relieved that Henry failed to seduce Kayley? I guess it means that she actually does need to be seduced, not just propositioned, he thought.

Intrigued, unable to fathom her, he felt a need to see her that instant. He walked through the house and around the garden looking for her but she wasn't there. Henry was nowhere to be found either. He walked out to the driveway. Henry's car was gone and his heart sank.

5

Kieran sat at his desk in his room all afternoon waiting for Henry and Kayley to return. He could hardly move let alone work. Frozen, numbed, he looked at his computer screen, flitting from website to website.

The Irish Times, nothing to read, the Guardian, nope, the New York Times, same headlines as all the rest, the Telegraph, Express, shock horror probes, scandal, romping royals, insane politicians. It made him feel no better to flick from one news outlet to the next. Like eating junk food, always desiring fulfilment, but never finding it, nevertheless the addict continues to search for satisfaction in the same failed remedies.

He could not look at the script or his new story, nothing until he knew if Henry had succeeded in seducing Kayley. The hours gnawed at his psyche, twisting his thoughts. He felt unable to think, 'How could I have been so stupid?' he wondered.

As afternoon turned into evening his nervousness fell into a dreary resignation. I have missed my chance at happiness. I let my best friend steal the love of my life, he wailed inside.

As dusk set in he had a glass of wine and his mood changed. After the third glass he began to feel a bit more like himself. Oh well, never mind, I didn't really fancy Kayley at all, he rationalised.

At last he worked up enough courage to check his email after a seven-hour hiatus. Sure enough, Zak had sent him five new emails. He immersed himself in the intricate details of how he was going to direct the scene when the female Viking zombies (the un-dead Shield Maidens) were to rape a group of living Irish monks and make it seem realistic.

His mind ablaze, his head full of wine and now whiskey, he tapped frenetically at the keyboard with just one table lamp in the corner of his room to light the darkened house. He pulled at his unshaven chin, and scraped his fingers through his unwashed hair, eyes ablaze as he imagined zombie Valkyries devouring ...

Clunk, the front door shut. He heard two sets of footsteps and murmurs. He strained his ears to listen and he made out the sound of Henry saying, 'Well, there you are then.'

The footsteps clunked up the stairs and diverged at the landing, Henry going to his room and Kayley to hers. Two doors slammed shut.

At last freed from his torment, Kieran downed the last slug of his whiskey and, now satisfied, brushed his teeth, washed his face and went to bed.

He awoke with a terrible headache but checked his email. There was nothing from Zak. He felt sure he must be wearing him down by now. No one could keep up such a pace and expect other people to stay with them. At first Zak terrified him, now he felt he had his measure. Most of his incessant questions were repetitions of Zak's own fears. How will this work, what will the end result look like, will the producers 'give it love'?

As he made his way downstairs the fear and insecurity of the day before clawed its way through his hangover. He made his breakfast as usual, with a dose of two aspirin as an eye-opener.

Henry's door creaked open and he emerged hauling his suitcase. He dragged it down the stairs making a big clunk at each step. When he reached the bottom he looked up at Kieran, tortured.

'I am an artist,' he declared, 'I can no longer work under these oppressive conditions. I must, yes, I have no other recourse but to leave, at once! If I am not wanted I shall take my talents to where others, more knowing, will give me the appreciation my work deserves.' He raised his gaze to the ceiling, chin held out.

Kieran clapped his hands slowly, clap, clap, clap. 'Good performance, Henry.'

'All right ye bastard,' said Henry.

'Come and have heat of the tea,' said Kieran.

Henry made his breakfast and sat down with Kieran. 'I have my dignity intact,' he said. 'She's no lady. Well, she isn't perfect anyway.'

'Did she wrong you in some way, Henry?'

'No, no it's not that. It's just that she is incapable of understanding an artist like me. She is vapid, lifeless. She appreciates nothing of the subtleties of this world. I was wrong to see her in a more favourable light, as if she were more emotionally evolved. No, no, she is not worth the effort for me to educate her.'

'Henry, so what you are saying is that she wouldn't sleep with you?'

'No, of course, it's not that. Not at all. I have no need for sexual fulfilment, but I lust for spiritual enlightenment. That which she is incapable of understanding.'

They looked up as they heard Kayley's door open and her footsteps on the stairs. She came into the kitchen with a serene smile on her face, and a black pair of yoga pants and top.

'Good morning, Kayley. You look like a ninja,' Kieran smiled.

'Morning guys,' she said. 'You both look as if you're expecting something.'

'No Kayley, I have no more expectations of you,' said Henry, his eyes drooped down to the floor.

'Ah sure, don't be like that Henry, you know I respect you. I feel tenderness towards you in my own way and I love your painting,' Kayley said.

'My painting? What do you know of art? You will never grow to understand art, culture. You are too vain to understand the true meaning of art.'

'Now Henry, what way is that to talk to our guest? Don't be so judgemental,' said Kieran.

'You are right, the two of you - ganging up on me as you are. In any case, I have to get back to Dublin immediately. Then I think I'll book a flight to Malta. My brother and his family take a villa there every year at Gozo. It's great fun. Sun, cheap food and booze. You should try Malta some year, said Henry'

Kieran laughed inside and smiled as sweetly as he could, at Kayley. They finished their breakfasts, saying no more.

Henry hauled his bag, painting and easel into his car and drove over the hump down to Crookhaven and the road back to Dublin. Kayley and Kieran waved goodbye.

Now Kieran was left alone with Kayley. She looked sad and without a glance or word turned and strode back into the house and up to her room. Kieran heard her door slam shut and his heart fell.

He climbed the stairs back to his room and worked listlessly, replying to yet more emails from Zak. Zombies, I'm not sure I can relate to this anymore, he thought. I'm more interested in people who are alive.

He turned to his movie treatment, now titled 'The Eternal Sea', and worked on that instead. This title he felt sure captured the feeling of loss and melancholy that he was trying to convey. The sense of love unrequited, the cruelty of nature and the unremitting flow of time, the sea, love and waves.

Kieran gazed out his bedroom window to the west as the afternoon sun smothered the yellow gorse and purple heather with golden rays and dappled shadows. Low cumulus clouds danced across the landscape from west to east. Transfixed by the unfolding skyscape, he sat motionless as the twilight set in and the crimson clouds cast a magical glow across Inisheen.

Kayley at last came out of her room and tiptoed down to the kitchen. Kieran followed in his socks, no shoes, so as not to break the silent mood.

Still dressed in her ninja outfit, Kayley glanced over her shoulder at him.

'Sad are you, Kayley?' asked Kieran.

'Sad? Not at all. Why should I be sad?'

'Er, I dunno, I guess the house has been so quiet all day I felt a bit melancholy, you know, after Henry left like that.'

'Ah, don't worry about Henry, he's fine. Just a bit of a drama queen you know, don't you?

'Do you feel no remorse?'

'Remorse, are you kidding? We had a fun couple of days, messing around. What did you guys expect, that I would leave my husband and run away with him? Oh, that's right, I'm not married, but he is. So you think I'd be a home breaker?'

'I guess he expected more from you. You seemed to like him.'

'Kieran, he was chasing me, not the other way around. It's flattering to have someone show interest in you. Maybe guys don't understand that because they are usually the chasers, not the ones being chased.'

Kieran felt humbled, caught out. It was true that he and Henry had considered her fair game, to be seduced if not hunted. 'You are right, Kayley, we've not shown that much interest in you, in who you are. Only in what you are, which is a fascinating and beautiful woman.'

She smiled at him, 'There you go again, flirtation and flattery.' She laughed and sat down at the kitchen table.

'So what's this important movie you're working on,?'
'It's called 'Vikings: Zombies Awake'.'
'Zombie Vikings? You're pulling me leg aren't ye?'
'Not at all, it's going to be a big hit.'
'Why zombies?'
'Well, zombie films are one of the constants in Hollywood. Ever since 'White Zombie' in 1932 there have been numerous zombie movies, and now is the time for the next one.'
'How do you mean?'
'Studios are always looking years ahead at their release schedules. They go through cycles of genres. You know werewolf, vampire movies. Zombie movies always sell but you can't do them every year. Their data steered them to the conclusion that next year is perfect for the next zombie wave.'
'Sounds like looking into tea leaves.'
'It is, but driven by research, focus groups, group psychology, data, but most importantly, money.'
'Why Vikings?'
''Return of the Viking' was a hit series. It spawned several shows along the same lines. You know, hunky guys chopping off heads and Valkyrie-like women, sex, adventure. It's a perfect dramatic mix.'
'So the data say, next year is Vikings and zombies?'
'Exactly. The only trouble is that often several studios come to the same conclusion at the same time. So there is always a danger that you end up with three movies in a similar genre in the same year. As far as we know, we are the only zombie movie going into production this year. So the road is clear and we are expecting it to be a big hit.'
'As a film school graduate, it seems disappointingly un-artistic to just repeat the same old formulas.'
'Perhaps, but a lot of artistry and craft will go into making the film. Zak Flender has never made a film that didn't make money, and he has two hits under his belt.'
'So it's all about the money?'
'At this level for sure. But art is always driven by money, isn't it? If it weren't for the Catholic Church, there would be no European art history. The same is true for eastern art – religious patronage was the driving force. I mean, they had the resources to pay for artisans, sculptors,

painters, draftsmen. Nowadays it's commerce, capital that provides the impetus for artistic endeavours.'

'You sound like one of my lecturers. Perhaps that's what you should do, teach art history.'

'Thanks Kayley. I hope I can still do, not just teach.'

'Oh well, your lecture sent me to sleep. Now I have to go and lie down. I'll have an essay ready for you tomorrow,' said Kayley.

'Don't be like that, Kayley. Stay and we can cook dinner together.'

'Fine. I'll cook my food and you can make yours.'

They began to prepare their evening meals, Kayley on one side of the island counter and Kieran opposite her.

'Who was your friend with the Mercedes?' he asked her.

'He was in my class at uni and we were together for a while. He did his last year at a film school in Germany, so we split up, both agreeing it was best. We're still friends though, nothing serious at all. I just saw him for old times sake.'

'What about the other boys?'

'Ah, just guys I met down here. Friends of friends. Everyone is on summer holidays.'

She sliced vegetables slowly, her eyes transfixed on her task as she picked up a carrot, examined it and gently cut it, as if creating a work of art. Kieran could not concentrate on his preparations, but glanced at her, taking in the shape of her eyes, the colour of her auburn hair, the pout of her lips. Her long hair fell over her blushed cheeks and black tight-fitting top. Her fingers were long and slender. Her demeanour was so confident, serene.

After a while, she stopped knife in hand and looked at him. 'Why are you staring at me?'

'Oh, pardon me, I'm not, it's just that, well I am writing an outline for a movie, and I've based a character on you.'

'On me? What do I do in the film?'

'Do? Nothing as yet, I mean I haven't got very far. It's still mostly an idea.'

'An idea? Well, what role to I play? You must know that at least.'

'You're the … love interest.'

'The female love interest, you mean? It takes two to tango, doesn't it.'

'Yes, yes of course. There is a man involved, it is a binary story, you know what I mean.'

'So who is the male love interest based on?'

'Ah, no one real, just a flawed character, an invention.'

'But my character can't be based on me. After all, you hardly know me.'

'True, I guess it was the impression that you gave me, the feeling I got that stuck with me when you first arrived. Somehow I was inspired and the mix of feeling, mood and emotion transformed into a character in my mind.'

'I'm surprised you have time for personal writing with your work on Zombies: The End Game.'

'It's called 'Vikings: Zombies Awake' actually. But they are intending for this film to be one of a series, if it's successful. Anyway, I'm not meant to be working on it full time while I'm here. This is supposed to be a getaway before we start production in September.'

'I'll be interested to hear how my character turns out. What's her name?'

'No name yet. But what about Helen?'

'Helen of Troy? The face that launched a thousand ships?'

'Yes, that's perfect. The movie does have an ocean theme.'

They were silent for a while each concentrating on their cooking.

Kieran said, 'I would like to get to know you, I mean to help me with the characterisation.'

'All right, but we shall have to be careful. Your story will fall apart if the male lead turns out to be based on you.'

'No, no, it's not me at all. I promise to be just your friend. I'm not like Henry.'

'Do you mean you're not married, or not a chat-up artist?'

'Both, I mean neither. I'm not married.'

'Nor betrothed?

'No, not that either.'

'Ah, all right then, Sir Galahad. Let's be friends. Purely platonic relationship. That way I can relax while I'm here on me holliers and not worry about being chased by flattering, flirting men who have but one thing on their minds.'

6

Kieran awoke as usual and set to work preparing notes for the VFX supervisor. He needed to give him all the details of the scene of the zombies marching and attacking the castle so his team could prepare their work. The supervisor was a senior artist working from one of the major visual effects vendors in Soho. He had won an Emmy and been nominated for a BAFTA for previous films.

The VFX crew would be doing their own shoot in tandem with Kieran's cinematography team. They would cover the whole set with cameras. They needed to capture the position of everyone on set, actors and all of the camera crew, the lighting and textures of everything. They would recreate the entire set in three dimensions in software, and use it as a base to create computer graphic imagery to supplement or replace elements, including the main characters, and extend the set. Once the shots were complete, it was possible that little of Kieran's material would end up in the final released movie.

He could hardly concentrate on this detailed work. His mind in turmoil. What a fool I am. I let Henry beat me to her and he spoiled my chances. Now I've agreed to be her friend, he thought.

He had never won over a woman by pretending he wasn't interested in her. That was something only actors in movies could do. He couldn't play the aloof artist, heroin eyes, distanced gaze and hope that eventually she would throw herself at him, madly in love. No, he was going to have to win her over, but he had promised he wouldn't chase her. Unsure how to proceed, he finished his work and went down for a late breakfast.

'Good morning,' chirruped Kayley. 'What are you up to today? Working the whole time?'

'No, I just finished work on Zombie for the day. I could work on my story, or we could go on a drive if you like?'

'Let's go to the beach. I can read my book and we can enjoy the sunshine.'

Kieran drove them to Barleycove and they placed two big towels on the sand. Kayley took off her blouse and shorts to reveal her svelte figure and bikini for the first time.

The water was too cold for more than a quick dip, but Kieran acted playfully, splashing water at her. They ran back up the sand and crashed onto their towels.

Droplets of water slid down her back and shoulders as if caressing her skin. Kieran couldn't bear to look and turned and laid on his side. Soon Kayley propped herself up and opened her book. Kieran glanced over his shoulder. She was reading the screenplay of the Éric Rohmer film 'Love in the Afternoon'.

'Why are you reading that?' He asked.

'Josh gave it to me. He said if I wanted to be a filmmaker I had to read it as soon as possible.'

'How do you know Josh anyway?'

'He was a guest lecturer at my uni.'

'You had a thing with him?

'We just became friendly.'

'Josh is married, you know?'

'I'm not going to break his home. It's just a casual relationship. He's an interesting man.'

Kieran sighed to himself in resignation. 'There are lots of interesting people in this business, but you should be careful.'

'I thought you and Josh were friends,' said Kayley

'We are friends, but our relationship is unequal in nature. He is rich and successful and I am, so far, a nobody.'

'Then why does he act like your friend?

'Because I'm in the industry and I'm on the inside. But you learn not to take people too seriously. Everyone is friendly in the movie business. It's the nature of the business. There are talented people, egos, sensitivities. People are in show business to express themselves, and they seek affirmation. Everyone wants to be appreciated, loved. So everyone is friendly. But eventually the power dynamics of the relationships come to the fore.'

'So you think Josh will dump you someday?'

'If this movie goes well and I gain in stature, maybe not. Maybe we'll be more equal and our friendship will grow. I'm not suggesting he's disingenuous. It's the way of the world. Like the prince and the pauper. The prince will be whisked away one day, his attention demanded by others. The pauper, or showgirl, will be left behind and be just a pleasant memory to him.'

'So I shouldn't try and rise above my station?'

'Just be careful. I don't want you to get hurt.'

'Don't be silly. I can look after myself better than you think.'

'Perhaps you can, but people wonder why show business people have so many marriages and lovers. I think it's because, for them, it's all about the story. That's what they live and breathe, and why they're in the business in the first place. As kids they spent their time daydreaming. All kids daydream, but for people who become actors, singers, cameramen, directors, make-up artists, the story becomes who they are. They turn everything in their lives into a little scenario, a story. They can't help it.

'They meet someone and imagine a picture perfect life. They create a tableau in their minds and think yes, that's going to be great. Of course, the reality turns out differently, especially if two show folk get together. They each have a little scene that they are acting out – a double fantasy. In the end, it breaks apart because there was nothing holding it together in the first place – just a fantasy. Or they lose interest in the story and when someone else comes along they create a new one. They don't do it consciously. They just can't help themselves.

'So you have to be careful, giving yourself, your love. Your lover may be here today and off to another show tomorrow.'

'You are nice to worry about me. It's very sweet of you. It's like you're my best friend.'

Kieran's heart sank. He had heard the three worst words a girl could say to a boy, nice, sweet, friend. It was clear to him now that he had not created any sparks with Kayley. Her lips didn't tingle at the thought of his embrace. He became resigned to his status of a friendly chaperone.

After a while, Kayley glanced up from her book and said, 'Tell me about the story you're writing.'

'It's a love story, a bit like 'Gone with the Wind'.'

'Oh, a big costume drama epic set in wartime.'

'No, no, just the tension between the two main characters. They are destined for one another but circumstances prevent them from staying together.'

'Or is it more like Casablanca? They meet, fall in love but are torn apart.'

'Now that's a good idea, I like that. But maybe more like 'Titanic'. The lovers were from different backgrounds, so they were forbidden to be together. But they fell in love anyway.'

'In the end they are separated in a big dramatic scene when the ship sinks?'

'Actually, at the end of my story they sail away, leaving the world they knew behind to be together.'

'Like 'The Graduate'?'

'Yeah, that's a good ending.'

''The Graduate' was a romantic comedy. At least that was the genre the film critics squeezed it into. Is that what your story is?'

'Not really. I don't think I can do comedy. It's more of a coming of age romance perhaps.'

'Ah, so they're teenagers like, 'Romeo and Juliet.'

'I'm not sure, but I do have an atmosphere and a look in my mind.'

'Where are you up to? Do you have an ending?'

'I'm working on creating the tension between the two main characters. There has to be a challenge to overcome. She can't just fall into his arms.'

'Maybe when they first meet he's dismissive of her. After all, they are from different backgrounds, so the boy doesn't notice the girl at first,' suggested Kayley.

'Maybe the tension comes because they are at different stages in life.'

'Oh, like you and me?'

'You're right. It is as if we are on different rungs of the same ladder. I didn't want to push you away when we first met. I was wrapped up in my own journey. But I felt attracted to you.'

'I thought you decided I wasn't worth the effort. You were right, of course. I'm too young for you, inexperienced. Just a silly graduate looking for a start. You're a successful cinematographer, now to be a director.'

'But I liked you right away. I thought you were beautiful and intriguing. I don't think we are that different and our age doesn't matter. I'm not that much older than you.'

'But we're just friends Kieran. I like you, I do. Maybe I can help you. We can work on the story together.'

'No, Kayley, this is a personal endeavour. What is your ambition in film making anyway? Do you want to write, produce?'

'I see myself directing. But maybe the best way into the industry is through producing. There seem to be a lot of female producers. Maybe I can get a junior role somewhere.'

'Where are you from, you sound like you're from Cork.'

'I'm from Dublin, but my parents moved to Cork so they could afford a better place. They commute to Dublin or London when they get work. My father is a musician.'

'Playing in a band?

'Yes, lots of bands. But for money, he works as a session musician, mostly for TV and commercials. He's worked on film soundtracks as well.'

'What about your mother?'

'She's a painter. But for money, she's a production designer and does bits and bobs on film sets. They both take whatever work they can get.'

'So your family are in the industry. Well, there you are. So that's why you studied film.'

'I guess so. My parents sent me to music and dance lessons. Early on I took up acting and I did two years at a drama school in England before uni. But I'm more interested in the whole creative process, how movies are put together.'

He was astonished at his naivety. He had been giving her advice about show folk and she was from a show family. He felt foolish, but his fascination with her grew with every word she said. She wasn't just vivacious and attractive. She was intelligent, driven and talented.

'So what will you do with your story? Will you write a synopsis and treatment and tout it around to see if you can get development funding?'

'You're one step ahead of me all the way, Kayley. I'm down here to work on Zombie. My story is just an idea that came into my mind. But you're right. If it's going to get anywhere I'd better get serious and map out its trajectory.'

Kieran and Kayley were inseparable from then on. For the next few days, they ate breakfast, lunch and dinner together and read by the fire at night. They went for walks across the hills and swam at Barleycove.

After Henry had tried to seduce her, Kieran felt he had to rise to the challenge and was determined to have her. But now, he felt a pang in his heart as he thought of her. Whenever he glanced up and saw her face a thrill of excitement tingled through him and his pulse jumped. She is a vision he thought, but so much more. She is a talent, a bright, beautiful personality. Now he wanted her love, not for her to simply to fall for his charms.

Kieran played the role of a perfect gentleman, turning his back when Kayley took off her bikini and put on her clothes for the drive back up to Inisheen from the beach. Actually, he did have a few quick glances at her teardrop breasts.

At night they kissed on each cheek French style and went to their separate rooms.

'Good night Kieran,' Kayley called from her bed.

'Good night Kayley,' Kieran called back.

7

The next morning there was just one email from Zak
It read, 'Kieran, some more of the crew have arrived from LA.
Come over to my house this afternoon, I want you to meet the production
designer and the VFX producer will be here as well. A casual get to know
each other. We'll have a drink on the lawn.'

At breakfast he said, 'Kayley, I have to go out this afternoon.'

'Oh, can I come?'

'Zak invited, I mean commanded, me to go over to see him at his
house near Bantry.'

'So it's work.'

'I guess so. He said we would have a drink on the lawn.'

'Go on, bring me along. You can have a drink and I'll drive us home,'
said Kayley.

It seemed a good idea to have a non-drinking driver. But he wondered
about Kayley's motives. 'I think Zak might be gay you know, Kayley.'

'Don't be silly. I'm not interested in Zak, although I've never met him.
But I would like to see the big house and meet some industry people,' she
said.

Kieran had no idea at all if Zak was gay. He had met him several times
as well as seen him on a few video calls. He had big arm muscles and
clearly worked out, unlike Kieran. He had a few tattoos and piercings. He
seemed neat and tasteful, but that didn't mean he was gay.

In the late afternoon they set out for Bantry in Kieran's car. The drive
took a little over half an hour. They drove past the statue of St Brendan
on the town square by the harbour as Kieran followed the purple line on
his satnav along the coast road.

Just outside Bantry they noticed a sign, 'Kilnaruane Pillar Stone'.

Kayley said, 'Please let's stop and have a look.'

They pulled over and walked up a muddy path into a field. In the middle of the field was a cordoned off area and a stone pillar about two metres tall. They went up close and walked around it, examining its carved surface. There was a carving of a boat, a currach, being rowed by four oarsmen and a helmsman. They were surrounded by crosses as if floating in the sea.

'It looks like Saint Brendan. What a great story that is. I'd like to make that movie. A group of monks led by a visionary, sail off across uncharted oceans in search of paradise, but find America instead,' said Kieran.

They returned to the car and continued on the road. 'There it is,' said Kayley pointing to a big Georgian house at the top of a long driveway surrounded by large ornamental gardens. Kieran stopped at the imposing iron entry gates.

'Maybe he's staying in the cottage out the back,' Kayley laughed.

'I think not. I have to ring the bell.'

He pushed the buzzer and after a few moments the gates swung open and they continued up the driveway. He stopped the car in front of the large stoop that led to a portico and double front doors.

Before they could get out of the car a man in a tweed jacket emerged from a side door and waved at Kieran urging him to drive the car over to him and said, 'You can't park there, for heaven's sake, not in that.'

He directed them to a side parking area with a sign that read - Tradesman's Entrance. 'I should have rented a Merc for this,' Kieran mumbled.

The man ushered them in at the tradesman's door and through the kitchen into the entrance hall of the house. 'Wait here,' he said. They stood and admired the handsome double semi-circular staircase that wound its way up three floors. Above, inside a dome painted powder blue, light gleamed in through stained glass windows.

'Impressive, Kieran, but we don't even warrant the front door,' Kayley teased him with a big grin on her face.

Soon a maid came and waving her hand as if they were naughty children shooed them out to the back of the house through a magnificent double living area with two huge fireplaces, multiple leather sofas, tall oak bookcases filled with expensive leather-bound volumes and major artworks on the walls. She lead them out through floor-to-ceiling glass doors onto a large, wide, immaculate lawn tastefully decorated with ornamental shrubs and formal flower beds. It overlooked Bantry Bay with a magnificent view of the mountains of the Beara Penninsula across the bay.

Set off to one side was a white wrought iron table and eight chairs where several people were lounging. Zak stood up and walked over to greet them.

'Kieran, so glad to have you here,' he said. He smiled at Kayley looking her up and down.

'Zak, may I present my friend Kayley. She is staying with me. I hope you don't mind.'

'Very pleased to meet you, Kayley,' he said, ignoring Kieran. Smiling he bent his arm for her to hold and arm in arm they walked towards the table with Kieran following.

Nope, he doesn't seem gay to me. Not at all, he thought cursing his bad decision making once again.

'Hey Kieran,' said Melanie, the VFX producer from Soho.

'Melanie!, muah, muah.' They kissed each other on the cheek.

'This is Lukasz, the production designer. I don't think you've met as yet.'

'Hi Lukasz, no, we haven't met. I don't think you were around when I was in LA,' said Kieran.

'Yesh, Kiera-a-a-n, zhach is correct, I was in Budapest working on *Barbarians: The Coming*,' intoned Lukasz in a thick Polish accent.

Zak and Kayley continued to the end of the garden admiring the view and chatting. Kieran sat down and a waitress brought him an electric blue drink in a wide glass.

'Here you are, sir, a Cobalt Daquiri,' she said. Kieran grimaced and she said. 'Can I get you something else?'

'Champagne, please,' said Kieran his eyes fixed on Zak and Kayley.

He chatted with Lukasz and Melanie and guzzled champagne. The waitress was very attentive and his glass never seemed to be more than half empty. After what seemed a long time, Zak and Kayley came over to the table and joined them. As the sun went down behind the distant clouds in the southwest the sky radiated gold, then pink and finally a tequila sunrise red as the Beara Peninsula fell into darkness.

Kieran became engaged in a long conversation, almost impossible to understand, with Lukasz. The champagne made him animated, he waved his arms in explanation and nodded his head vigorously in agreement with whatever Lukasz said.

As darkness finally took hold, Zak stood up. 'Well everyone, thank you for a very enjoyable mixer this evening. We have work to do tomorrow so I think we should all get going.'

The soiree was over and Zak ushered Kieran and Kayley into the house. Kieran was fearful he might shove them out the tradesman's entrance and was relieved when he walked them to the front door, which the maid opened for them.

As they were leaving he said, 'I'm having a party here tomorrow night. More of the crew will be coming down from Dublin so you must come, and please be sure to bring Kayley,' he said smiling at her. 'There are plenty of rooms here for you both to stay, so no need to worry about driving home after drinking. See you tomorrow.'

Kieran slumped in the passenger seat as Kayley drove them back to Inisheen. 'You and Zak certainly got on well,' he said.

'Yes, he is a very interesting man,' said Kayley.

She drove with confidence. Kieran kept looking at the side of her face, her features were so clear, streaking from shadow to dark as lights of cars and houses flashed by.

As they climbed the stairs to their rooms he put his arm around her waist and she turned to him. Her eyes stared into his and her lips pouted. They kissed and embraced. He said, 'I can't help myself, I've fallen for you.'

'You're very nice, Kieran. I like you a lot, too much maybe,' she said.

They kissed again, but she soon pulled away. 'You should get some sleep Kieran, get the champagne out of your system. Good night.'

She disappeared into her room leaving Kieran's emotions and body tangled in his desire for her.

While Kieran was checking his email the next morning he regretted kissing Kayley. He felt he had let his guard down, given away his feelings too stridently. But she hadn't pushed him away. She had kissed him back. Was he reading the signs correctly he wondered?

He went downstairs and Kayley was making breakfast wearing a t-shirt and bare legs. After breakfast he said, 'I'm sorry about last night Kayley. The champagne did get to me I suppose, but in vino veritas.'

'Don't worry, Kieran, your attention is flattering. I can't help liking it. You've been good company for the last few days. I've enjoyed our time together.'

Could it be that she was falling for him he wondered? Maybe she wasn't in love with him, but falling for his charm would be fine with him after all.

He put his hand gently in hers and she squeezed his fingers. 'I feel like you've been courting me like a real gentleman.' she said.

'Not going too fast for you I hope?'

'No, not too fast.'

He moved closer to her and went to kiss her but she moved her face away.

'I'm still not ready, Kieran, but I feel something for you now.'

'You're a mysterious woman, Kayley. You seemed so passionate with those other guys. I think we can risk some intimacy.'

'Not now, not today. It's different with people of my own age, from the same year at uni. Somehow it's natural, casual. With you, it seems more serious. I need to take my time. But we have time, don't we? Let's see how we feel after the party tonight. I'm looking forward to that.'

Kieran determined to play his part and stay the gentleman. He was nice and entertaining for the rest of the day. They played badminton in the garden and lazed on deck chairs. The afternoon wore on and the time came to go to the party.

They each packed an overnight bag and Kieran drove, this time he knew where to park. They walked around the house to the front steps and went in through the main door. From the entrance hall, Kieran could see a drinks table in the living room and made straight for it. He picked up two glasses of champagne and turned around to find Kayley. She was still at the front door and waved for him to come over.

'Come on, we have to be shown our rooms first,' she said. The maid took them upstairs and showed them two adjoining bedrooms. 'I'll get the bags from the car, you don't need to worry, I'll meet you inside' said Kayley.

Kieran wandered through the living rooms and out into the garden still with a glass in each hand. The first one was now empty and he set it down. There were already a few dozen people talking, drinking and eating canapés.

'Hi Kieran, come and meet my team,' said a big man with a full beard. It was Jordan the Director of Photography. He was standing with several guys dress in plaid shirts and big shoes. One of them slapped him on the back and said, 'I'm so looking forward to working with you, I love your work.'

Several glasses of champagne later there was a brief moment of silence. Jordan leaned over to him and said softly, 'I'm sorry. In my opinion it's unfair. I just wanted you to know.'

'Unfair? What are you talking about Jordan?'

'Bringing in Lars. I think it's unnecessary, and not fair to you.'

'Lars? You don't mean Lars Halkonen, do you? Nobody mentioned him to me.'

'You haven't heard? Well maybe it's just a rumour then. I'm relieved, like I said, I'm against it. So I'm glad I was wrong.'

'Where did you hear that Jordan?'

'Actually Kieran, I don't remember. Rumours, that's all. You hear all kinds of bullshit in this business. I'm looking forward to working with you. Cheers.'

They clinked glasses and Kieran gulped his champagne. 'Hey Jordan, I'm going to walk around a bit, see you later.'

He felt unnerved and confused. He was dizzy, his heart racing and hot flushes pulsed through his face. I knew it, I knew I couldn't trust that bastard Zak.

Lars Halkonen had been Assistant Director on 'Barbarians: The Coming'. So Lukasz and Melanie must have known. Everyone knows but me. That must be why he invited me over for drinks last night. He was going to tell me then, but the rat started hitting on Kayley instead. Damn coward. At least he didn't fire me by email or text.

He picked up another glass of champagne and went out to the lawn. He hadn't seen Kayley since she went to the car and he wandered around looking for her.

The party was in full swing and a band set up on the lawn and started playing. The singer belted out in a Cork accent, 'Brown Sugar, how come you taste so good, ooh, yea.' The crowd cheered and dancers swept onto the lawn swirling to the old beat. Actually, they are quite good dancers, thought Kieran. That's what you get with show folk, they aren't shy and they're talented.

With drink in hand Kieran wandered all over the house looking for Kayley, and Zak, but caught sight of neither of them.

In a corridor on the second floor, he bumped into one of the line producers. 'Hi Kieran, I'm sorry to hear the news man,' he said and continued on down the corridor patting Kieran on the back as he went. That's the second time tonight someone's patted me on the back. Now he felt rage building up inside of him.

Angry, he wandered through the house. On the top floor, he heard voices in a room with its door ajar. He heard Kayley laugh. He pushed the door open and to see Zak and a small group of people including Kayley, sitting on sofas around a glass coffee table. It looked as if, yes, they were doing lines. As he approached someone tossed a magazine onto the table covering up whatever was going on.

Kayley looked at him, her eyes bright, a big smile on her face. Zak said, 'Hey Kieran, how are you doing? You look a bit wiped out sport. Maybe you need a break.'

'Zak, I need to talk to you,' said Kieran.

'Sure, let's take breakfast together in the morning,'

'I mean right now Zak, now, I have to talk to you,' said Kieran, his eyes glaring.

Zak seemed to get the message, nodded and stood up. 'Let's go out on the balcony, I have a few minutes.'

They walked through a pair of French doors onto a balcony that looked down on the front garden and driveway, facing away from the raging party at the back of the mansion. The sounds of the band playing 'Knights in White Satin' reverberated around the gardens.

'What's on your mind, Kieran?'

'Zak, are the rumours true?'

'The rumours are always true.'

'So you're replacing me with Lars Halkonen?'

'No, not replacing you. I'm just bringing him onboard.'

'Why?'

'Because he's a comer. You're a comer, don't worry.'

'I'm not working for Lars, no way.'

'No, you're not. You work for me.'

'Then why bring him in? Three's a crowd.'

'He's available, that's why. I think he'll bring something to the show, add a new dimension to what we're doing. Besides, it'll keep the producers quiet. You're an unknown quantity and he has a track record. The money is a very important part of the process, as you are aware.'

'What's he going to do? What will I be left with?'

'We still have to figure that out, but we have time. I've been pleased with the progress we've made together here. We've gotten through it all much quicker than I expected. We can work through everything. Just stay cool, got it? I gotta go back into my guests now.'

'Your guests? I came here with Kayley.'

'Yes, but you two aren't together are you? I mean you're not an item. She's sharing Josh's house with you, right?'

'What's your interest in her Zak?'

'No interest, or lots of interest. It's not your place to ask. She's a talented girl, I like her.'

'That's right Zak, she's a girl.'

'I mean woman, she's not a teenager. She is an adult and she can look after herself. Besides, Josh and I are friends. I told him I'd look after her. She'll be fine. But you? Frankly, you look a mess. You ought to go sleep it off. As I said, let's do breakfast, all right?'

Kieran turned around and went back into the room. Kayley was in earnest conversation with a guy with a topknot. 'Kayley, come on let's go,' he said slowly.

'Go? Kieran, you go. You look like you need a lie-down. I'm fine, I'll catch up with you later or in the morning.' She returned to her conversation.

Kieran felt helpless and marched out of the room and down the stairs. He picked up an unopened bottle of champagne and continued out the front door and into his car.

He drove through the town of Bantry as carefully as he could. There was a Garda patrol stopped on the high street. The two Gardaí looked at him as he drove past but they didn't move.

He arrived home and opened the champagne. He awoke in the middle of the night, his head in his arms on his table, and stumbled onto his bed.

8

Twillip- twillip twillip-twillip. He was still in his clothes and he fished his phone out of his pocket. 'Yeragh, hello ... Kayley, where are you? ... Oh at the house where I left you of course ... No, I didn't abandon you ... Well I'm sorry if you feel abandoned. You seemed to be having a good time ... Alright alright, I'll come and get you as soon as possible. See you in forty-five minutes or so ... You were worried about me? ... That's wonderful to hear, but I'm grand thanks be. See you soon.'

Kieran had a quick shower and put on clean clothes. He was about to leave but changed his mind and took his shirt off. I should have a shave. After my performance last night I'd better be on my best form, he thought.

Clean and sooth he drove down the road to Bantry once more. He felt pleasantly surprised that Kayley had said she was worried about him. She genuinely seemed to care about him. He drove into the side car park again. The side door of the house was open so he went in that way. 'Morning all,' he beamed at the staff as he paraded through the kitchen and into the entrance hall.

He saw a group of people on the back lawn having brunch, and spotted Zak. He texted Kayley and she came downstairs with her bag over her shoulder, carrying Kieran's overnight bag in her arms.

'All recovered from last night?' she asked.

'I'm fine. Let's get of here, but first I need to see Zak. Wait in the car for me, I'll only be a minute,' said Kieran.

He put on a big smile and walked nonchalantly into the garden. Zak was serving himself what looked like kedgeree from a silver bain-maire.

'Kieran, you're looking surprisingly dapper and well this morning,' said Zak.

'I was a bit under the weather yesterday. I had terrible hay fever, I was sneezing and weeping all day. But today I'm fine. That's the summer weather for you. It was a great party last night. Ah it was, and thanks for your hospitality. Next time don't have so much champagne perhaps. Go on, it was a grand evening.'

'That's nice, thank you, Kieran. You seemed a bit upset last night, but you seem very cool now.'

'Zak, me upset? No no, it was the terrible hay fever that was afflicting me so. Today I have perfectly clear vision. I can see all the way to Kerry. Actually I can see all the way to Kerry from here. Fantastic place you found. I should have mentioned that earlier.'

'Yea, it's wonderful, isn't it? Last year I was in Romania, but Ireland is so much more interesting. You know, I love your country. The people are so friendly.'

'Friendly and talented Zak, don't forget that. Also, us locals, we know the lie of the land, you know. We know where the best locations are, the time of day, inside knowledge. That can never be underestimated.'

'Of course not, we value what the local crew can bring to the project. I'm counting on you Kieran, I need you.'

'Do you also need Lars Halkonen?'

'Yes, I do, as I explained. He'll keep the heat off my back. But don't worry so much Kieran. You're the main guy, my point man. Don't screw up a good thing.'

'I won't Zak. You can rely on me, that's for sure. I'm here for you night and day. I'll deliver your vision for you. You have my word.'

'Kieran, I knew about you. I had an instinct, a hunch. You know how to play the scene, the way to go. By the way, you have taste as well. I mean Kayley, she's special. You have an eye for talent.'

'You like her, do you?'

'Yes I do. You make sure she's on set. Give her a role of some kind.'

'Zak, I've no problem with that or anything. As you said, we'll work through it all.'

'Let's take a few days off. I'll talk to you later in the week.'

Kieran's hands were on fire as he marched away from Zak through the house and out the big front door, down the stoop and around to the tradesman's car park. He hadn't even been aware that Josh knew Zak. But of course, Josh knows everybody, he thought. He felt as if he had been set up by the three of them, Josh, Kayley and Zak.

Kieran felt energised by his talk with Zak, emboldened. No longer did he feel obliged to be polite, nice. He determined to take control.

In the car park, Kayley was leaning on the car staring at her phone. Without hesitation he demanded, 'Did you sleep with him?'

'None of your business, but no, of course not. Who do you think I am? I don't go to bed with just anyone. You guys have inflated ideas of yourselves. You have no morals. You judge women by your own low standards.'

'How can I believe you? You were coked up or worse.'

'I was not, I didn't do any drugs at all.'

'I saw, on the table, you were all doing lines of something.'

'You didn't see that at all. You were so drunk, how do you know what you saw? Talk about the pot calling the kettle black.'

'What about Josh? You had a thing with him too, didn't you? Did he tell you that Zak was going to be down here? Was this all a set-up with me as the mug?'

'No, I did not sleep with Josh. Yes, Josh mentioned that Zak would be down here. He told me that you would be here as well. He said that it wouldn't do any harm to be on holiday with some people in the industry. That if I were serious about my career, I should involve myself in the movie business and that it would be a waste of time to fritter my summer away in Greece drinking and dancing.'

'I didn't deceive anyone. I didn't ask any favours or make any promises. I'm just being myself and trying my best.'

'Are you telling me the truth? It's just that I care about you, for you. I only want to be with you.'

'Am I telling the truth? What about you, Kieran? Don't you have something to tell me? You said you weren't married.'

'I'm not.'

'Oh, well Henry told me ...'

'He told you about Cheryl?'

'Yes, you're engaged. So you don't only want to be with me, do you?'

'It's over between us, me and Cheryl. Why do you think I'm here all alone? I didn't want to burden you or Henry with my troubles. The truth is, I'm glad she broke it off. I was sad, but then I met you and I knew, for the first time, I really knew who I wanted. It's you Kayley, you're the one that I want. At least we can give it a try, can't we? I know now that you're attracted to me.'

'I am I suppose. But when I think of you cheating on your fiance and telling me who I can sleep with!'

'I should have told you earlier, I'm sorry. But I didn't want to be talking about another woman. I wanted to talk about you. I fell for you, head over heels. I came down here to be alone. You can ask Henry. He'll tell you that's what I told him when he showed up weeks early. I wasn't looking for another lover. I wanted peace, solitude. Then you arrived. I think it was meant to be, you and me.'

'So you've really split up with Cheryl?'

'It was a long time in the making. We haven't been lovers for ages. She was always working, making excuses. I've been alone for what seemed an eternity of wasted time, until I met you.'

He put his arms around her. She gently put one arm, then another around his shoulders. She buried her face in his chest. He combed his fingers through her long hair as if to soothe her. She looked up at him and they kissed.

'We must make love, otherwise, we'll never know if we were right for each other.'

'All right, Kieran. Let's go home.'

He drove once more down the road to Inisheen and at a fork in the road they were stopped by a herd of cows coming towards them. A car approached from the other fork with two young men inside. The driver was Michael, the boy that Kayley had been with at the house the previous week.

'Hey Kayley!' he shouted as he pulled his car up on the side of the road.

She opened the car door and went over to talk to them. She had her overnight bag over her shoulder just as she did when she got in the car. He couldn't tell whether it was by accident or design.

Kieran could half hear what they were saying over the mooing of the cows and the clip-clopping of their hooves along the road towards him.

'… we're going to Clonakilty, it's going to be a big night, come with us.'

'I'd love to but I can't. I'm with him.'

'Come with us. It's going to be a big party.'

'But I said I'd go with him.'

'Drop him. What do you want that old guy for?'

She continued talking to the boys, leaning in the window of the car. By now there was a queue of cars behind Kieran, eager to get going again. One of them leaned on the horn, drowning out what Kayley was saying.

The herd of cows reached a low point in the fence just ahead of his car and without hesitation, one by one they jumped over and into the field. At the back of the herd, the farmer kept them moving with a stick that he trailed on the ground behind them. Soon the last cow jumped into the field and the farmer tipped his hat to Kieran.

Kieran started the engine and felt his foot press on the accelerator. Soon he reached a bend in the road and he glanced in his rear view mirror to see Kayley still talking, oblivious that Kieran had gone. As he rounded the bend she fell out of view. He didn't know why he left her but he felt she would be fine with her friends. He had no plan, so he concentrated on the road ahead.

Soon he was pulling into the driveway of Inisheen. He went to his computer and searched various websites. Ah, perfect, he thought. A few clicks, then ping, the confirmation was in his email inbox. Another ping and he had received the boarding pass on his phone.

I should just about make it, he thought. He quickly packed up his things and threw his bag and computer into the car. He drove as fast as he dared, remembering how slowly he had driven through West Cork on his way down from Dublin. Now he hurried to get out. He didn't want to be late.

Just under two hours later, he left his car in the long-term car park at Cork Airport and found the departure lounge. He looked at the list of arrivals and departures. There is it, Aer Lingus, Cork to London Heathrow.

As he waited at the gate he read through his story. He had now figured out most of the plot points and many of the beats, but had yet to come up with a satisfactory ending. He had moved on from the misty boat scene at Crookhaven. He put various scenarios to test in his mind, rejecting each one in turn. He picks her up in his arms and carries her off into the night with flashes of light and smoke. No, no good. He gets down on one knee and proposes marriage. No, damn it.

What he did feel sure about was that the guy gets the girl and they set off into an unknown future full of love and hope. I guess I'll figure it out in London, he thought, and slapped his laptop shut.

His mind drifted back momentarily to Kayley and his time with her. It already seemed like a movie that he had seen last week. He knew it was a good movie but he struggled to remember the exact details.

He looked at the date on his smartwatch. It was two weeks and six days since he had walked with Cheryl on Killiney Strand.

****

Sean De Siun spent his early years in Australia before moving to London in the early 1970s.

His written works include non fiction redactions, documentaries, screenplays and short stories. He currently lives with his wife in Sydney Australia.

Also by the author and available
from Art Camino Fiction

Artists
Avatara
Kings Road
Desire
Caanice and the Book
Katie
Chatter

Copy Sales
Available on **amazon.com**
Purchase direct from **artcamino.com/fiction**